S0-BTA-285

Review Copy
Not for Resale
Mitchell Lane Publishers

RIVERS
OF THE WORLD

THE MISSISSIPPI RIVER

Claire O'Neal

Mitchell Lane
PUBLISHERS

P.O. Box 196
Hockessin, Delaware 19707

SOUTH HUNTINGTON
PUBLIC LIBRARY
HUNTINGTON STA.,NY
11746

J 977
O'Neal

RIVERS
OF THE WORLD

The Amazon River

The Nile River

The Ganges River

The Mississippi River

The Rhine River

The Tigris (Euphrates) River

The Yangtze River

The Volga River

Copyright © 2013 by Mitchell Lane Publishers

Printing   1   2   3   4   5   6   7   8   9

All rights reserved. No part of this book may be reproduced without written permission from the publisher. Printed and bound in the United States of America.

PUBLISHER'S NOTE: The facts on which the story in this book is based have been thoroughly researched. Documentation of such research can be found on page 44. While every possible effort has been made to ensure accuracy, the publisher will not assume liability for damages caused by inaccuracies in the data, and makes no warranty on the accuracy of the information contained herein.

**Library of Congress
Cataloging-in-Publication Data**
O'Neal, Claire.
  The Mississippi river / by Claire O'Neal.
     p. cm.—(Rivers of the world)
  Includes bibliographical references and index.
  ISBN 978-1-61228-296-1 (library bound)
  1. Mississippi River—Juvenile literature. I. Title.
  F351.O54 2012
  977—dc23
                                              2012009466

eBook ISBN: 9781612283692

PLB

CONTENTS

Schoolcraft State Park in
Minnesota is named after Henry
Schoolcraft, who discovered the
headwaters of the Mississippi
River in 1832.

CHAPTER 1

Big River: What's in a Name?

In July 1832, American explorer Henry Schoolcraft and his Ojibwe guide Ozawindib discovered the source of the Mississippi River. The mighty river began as a mere creek trickling away from a small lake in present-day Minnesota. The lake already had a name in two languages—Omushkos ("Elk Lake") to the Ojibwe tribe, and Lac la Biche ("Elk Lake") to French settlers. Knowing that it served as the source of the greatest river in the United States, Schoolcraft renamed it Lake Itasca, wordplay on the Latin phrase for "true head"—verITAS CAput.

For thousands of years, the people who lived and died by the river have struggled to put a name to this quietly powerful force of nature. To native tribes, it was the life-giving "Father of Waters." Sixteenth-century Spanish explorers called it "Escondido," a murky river full of hidden dangers.[1] Twentieth-century poet T.S. Eliot, a native of St. Louis, looked in its dirty, mysterious waters and saw a "strong, brown god." European settlers agreed with the Ojibwe tribe

Henry Rowe Schoolcraft (March 28, 1793 – December 10, 1864) was an American geographer, geologist, and ethnologist, noted for his early studies of Native American cultures, as well as for his 1832 expedition to the source of the Mississippi River.

of the northern Mississippi Valley when they called it "Mesipi," which simply means "Big River."

At Lake Itasca, Schoolcraft could jump across the Mississippi. By the time a drop from Lake Itasca reaches the river's mouth at Head of Passes, Louisiana—90 days and 2,340 river miles (3,779 kilometers) later—the Mississippi swells to one mile across and 45 feet deep. The wide, deep Old Man River swallows up tributaries—the Missouri, the Ohio, and the Arkansas Rivers—that are major rivers in their own right. The Ohio River is nearly as large as the Mississippi when they join at Cairo, Illinois. The Missouri River itself is the longest river in North

America at 2,540 miles (4,088 kilometers), traveling farther than the entire course of the Mississippi from its headwaters in Montana to its confluence with the Mississippi just north of St. Louis.

The Mississippi's "minor" tributaries aren't exactly minor either: the Illinois, the Tennessee, the White River in Arkansas, the Red River (which flows through Texas, Oklahoma, Arkansas, and Louisiana), and the Yazoo River in Mississippi. Add in the hundreds of thousands of streams, creeks, and seasonal water channels that discharge into the Mississippi and the result is a watershed that drains all the land between the Appalachians and the Rocky Mountains into the Gulf of Mexico, including 41% of the continental United States, and two Canadian provinces.[2]

Geographically, the Mississippi is so long that it is useful to think of it as two rivers, split in half where the Ohio River joins it at Cairo, Illinois. The Upper River, north of Cairo, cuts through bluffs and hillier lands as it flows through Minnesota, Wisconsin, Missouri, and Illinois. The river flows so wide through Minnesota and Wisconsin that it sometimes becomes a lake. Lake Pepin—the widest point of the Mississippi River—reaches over two miles across. The Upper River is so shallow—barely reaching a depth of 12 feet at Minneapolis—that islands build up in the middle of the river from deposited silt. Some can be several miles long, big enough to name.

South of Cairo, the Lower River carries a heavier load of water through very flat land. Its enormous volume gives the Mississippi strong currents that move in layers and whorls, making the river dangerous for small boats to navigate. The force of the river carves a deep bed, 170 feet below the water's surface at its deepest point in New Orleans. The riverbed even lies below sea level where it meets the Gulf, causing tides from the sea to spill upriver as far as 100 miles to Baton Rouge.

At Head of Passes, 90 river miles south of New Orleans, the river splits into many tiny streams called distributaries, which are smaller channels that branch off of the main body of the river. The channels turn southeastern Louisiana into a bayou, or swampland, overgrown

The river bustles with boat traffic in New Orleans. River barges float thousands of tons of goods like coal and grain up and down the river. A cross-river ferry carries cars and passengers across places where bridges can't be built.

with mangroves, cypress trees, and vines, and the home for crawfish and alligators. The river creeps through the bayou to the Gulf of Mexico, where its muddy brown waters dump fresh dirt, dulling the Gulf's pure blue in a four-mile-long smudge visible from space.

Those who know the Mississippi joke that the river has a mind of its own. Over its 1,800-mile course between Minneapolis and New Orleans, the river drops only 800 feet in elevation—an average of a mere few inches per river mile. The river flows slowly and lazily, moved only by the gentlest of tugs from gravity. Throughout the river's course it meanders, wandering slowly east and west like a coiling snake, hardly ever traveling directly south. From Lake Itasca, the Mississippi actually flows north for about 60 miles, then east toward Lake Superior, before heading south. The Lower River snakes the most, travelling the 600 miles between Cairo, Illinois and the Gulf of Mexico in nearly 1200 river miles. The Mississippi's meandering ways turn river water into knives, carving sediment from its banks. Topsoil, dirt, and silt also come to the river as runoff, carried over the flat river valley land by frequent rainstorms. The river moves this silt and soil as it flows, coloring the water with dirt and debris and giving the river its nickname. The Mississippi dumps over 100 million tons of sediment into the Gulf of Mexico every year, while depositing untold and even greater amounts on its banks and islands.

Measuring the exact length of the Mississippi is impossible because the river constantly shifts its course in tiny ways. During floods, the river pushes over itself, creating cut-offs, shortcutting its looping meanders. Abandoned loops can form oxbow lakes, or, over time, fill in with sediment to create new, flat land. When the river flows faster with spring rains, it might shift sideways, cutting into one bank faster than the other, dumping silt on the neglected bank. The town of Kaskaskia, Illinois, started on the east side of the Mississippi; after a flood in 1881,

The Dead Zone is where the Mississippi's polluted waters meet the Gulf of Mexico. Sea life avoids the oxygen-poor waters, which currently take up an area the size of New Jersey.

Keelboats and steamboats, seen in this historic drawing of New Madrid, Missouri, moved people and goods between river towns in early American history.

the river moved eastward. Now the town lies on Missouri land.[3] New Madrid, Missouri, has moved four times; its original site was in present-day Kentucky.

As one of the world's most navigable rivers—no rapids, dams, constrictions, or any other obstacles exist south of the Falls of St. Anthony in Minneapolis—the Mississippi played a crucial role in the history of the United States. Some of America's greatest cities, like Minneapolis, St. Louis, Memphis, and New Orleans grew up with their toes dangling into the Mississippi. The Mississippi River has acted as both a natural division between east and west, and a shared opportunity for north and south, as long as people have lived on its banks.

Earthquakes in Missouri?

Earthquake river damage

Earthquakes only happen in California, right? Actually, some of the strongest earthquakes in the continental U.S. have shaken the border between Missouri and Tennessee. Four earthquakes at magnitudes of nearly 8.0 each occurred during the winter of 1811-1812. Some shocks forced the Mississippi to run backward! Luckily, these powerful quakes caused relatively little damage to what was then a sparsely populated area.

The first earthquake hit near New Madrid, Missouri, on December 16, 1811. Residents reported loud noises like gunshots as the earth cracked open. From Cairo to Memphis, the Mississippi River rose up and battered its banks, as though a silent storm raged in the still air. Boats were tossed onto the riverbank like toys. The river seemed to swallow huge trees whole, and to shake off its normal banks like an old skin. The fourth and final major quake on February 7, 1812 sunk New Madrid so low that the Mississippi destroyed it, drowning residents and flooding buildings. Shaking sediments dammed the river on two sides in Tennessee, creating Reelfoot Lake.[4]

More than 200 earthquakes occur each year in the New Madrid Seismic Zone, but nearly all are too small to be felt by humans.[5] Geologists fear that the region is overdue for another large earthquake. With St. Louis and Memphis in striking distance, not to mention countless small towns, farms, and businesses throughout the area, this time the damage could be catastrophic.

The Middle Mississippian peoples, known as mound builders, built a capital city near modern-day Cahokia, Illinois. Monks Mound, the biggest mound in the New World, rises 100 feet (30 meters) in a series of terraces. Though 104 mounds remain at the site today, many more were leveled by early American settlers. Cahokia – one of only four prehistoric sites in the United States – was named a UNESCO World Heritage Site in 1982 to protect it from further damage.

CHAPTER 2

Father of Waters: Early History and Exploration

Geologically, the Mississippi River is young, formed about two million years ago by glaciers.[1] The river once ended at present-day Cairo, Illinois, where an ancient sea began. Sea levels dropped 21,000 years ago as towering glaciers grew to cover much of North America. As the coastline retreated slowly to its modern-day position at the Gulf of Mexico, the river followed, carving a path through the flat lands of Tennessee, Arkansas, Mississippi, and Louisiana. When the glaciers shrank about 12,000 years ago, they dumped huge, mineral-rich loads of pulverized rock onto the land and into the river, creating some of the most fertile soil in the world.

Civilization naturally arose and centered around the Mississippi River. By 800 CE, cities of early Mississippian peoples thrived with art, science, and trade along most of the Lower River, parts of the Upper River, and much of the Ohio River Valley.[2] Mississippian engineers oversaw construction of thousands of earthen mounds—many of which

This mural from the Cahokia site interpretive center depicts the city in its heyday. Cahokians enjoyed a life rich with art, games, and religion. Archaeologists have uncovered evidence of game fields, many temples, and even a wooden sun calendar, dubbed "Woodhenge" by archaeologists for its resemblance to Stonehenge in England.

remain today—for roads, flood control, or religious ceremonies. This sophisticated society built the largest prehistoric city north of Mexico near modern-day Cahokia, Illinois, which teemed with 20,000 residents at its height in the 11th century CE. No one knows why the Mississippian civilization suddenly and mysteriously collapsed around 1200 CE.

By the 16th century, Mississippians had reorganized into dozens of local tribes that lived independently of each other. Lower River tribes such as the Choctaw, Chickasaw, Natchez, Alabama, and Yaddo lived in flooded, swampy lands. They tilled the rich soil by hand to grow crops of maize, beans, squash, sweet potatoes, melons, and sunflowers. They made canoes from whole felled trees, with the heartwood dug out to make places to sit. Tribes who settled the Upper River, such as the Ojibwe (or Chippewa), Winnebago, Fox, and Sauk, favored flexible canoes made of birch bark. The lightweight canoes were ideal for traveling around reeds and grasses to gather wild rice, a staple of the Ojibwe diet, or for fishing or quietly hunting the elk that watered at lakes and rivers. Where streams and creeks ended—or even froze in the winter—native travelers could just pick up their boat and walk it to the next inlet.

The first European explorers to encounter the Mississippi River were uninterested and unprepared. On June 2, 1519, Spanish explorer Alonzo Álvarez de Pineda entered the Mississippi.[3] Álvarez de Pineda named the river Río de Espíritu Santo, or "River of the Holy Ghost," since his discovery fell on the Catholic holiday of Pentecost. It's unlikely that Álvarez de Pineda took his ship any distance up the river. Further exploration would have been a distraction from his primary mission, which was an effort to discover a possible shortcut to trading routes to China by mapping the coast of the Gulf of Mexico.

On May 8, 1541, Hernando de Soto encountered the river on foot, during his great overland expedition of North America. De Soto also sought a quick route to China, or gold, whichever came first. He and his men crossed the river near what is now Memphis, Tennessee. They quickly traveled beyond the Mississippi, fearing its dangerous waters and hostile natives. When de Soto died of fever on the trip back one year later, his men sank his body in the Mississippi.

The French approached the Mississippi with different intentions. Coming from New France in what is now eastern Canada, French "explorers" were often fur traders seeking new hunting territory, or Catholic priests looking for native souls to save. Like their native friends, they traveled light, in small boats or canoes well suited to the Mississippi, and especially to exploration of the Upper River. They learned native languages like Algonquin, which helped their chances of sharing the gospel – and surviving.

The first French team to explore the Mississippi was led by Louis Jolliet, a soldier and trader, and Father Jacques Marquette, a Roman Catholic priest. The pair and their small crew left from Marquette's church in Sault Ste. Marie on Lake Michigan on May 17, 1673, and portaged their light canoes to the Wisconsin River. Friendly Maskoutens natives they met along the way guided them to the Mississippi on June 17. Father Marquette wrote in his journal that safely reaching the great river filled him "with a Joy that I cannot Express."[4]

Jolliet and Marquette drifted along with the current for several months. Jolliet sketched maps as they went. He soon determined that the Mississippi did not head west to the Pacific as they had hoped, but rather south, towards the Gulf of Mexico. Father Marquette spoke several native languages and befriended the native tribes they met on

Father Jacques Marquette (1637-1675) was born in Laon, France, but made his home in France's New World territories. Marquette befriended native tribes, just as passionate to learn their languages and culture as he was to share Christianity. On their return voyage in late 1674, Marquette and Jolliet became the first Europeans to spend the winter in what is now the city of Chicago, as honored guests of the Illinois nation.

their journey. The Illinois in particular warned the explorers to turn back. Only misery awaited the French in the south, from heat, mosquitoes, and violent tribes. The natives also hinted that Spanish explorers had settled at the Mississippi's mouth. Rather than risk capture, Jolliet and Marquette turned back at the Arkansas River, returning to New France via the Illinois River.

The success of Jolliet and Marquette excited French explorer René-Robert Cavelier, also known as Sieur de La Salle. In 1682, de La Salle sailed south along the Mississippi from the Illinois River to the Gulf, claiming the river for France. De La Salle's partner, Louis Hennepin, sailed north from the Illinois until he reached the Falls of St. Anthony. Like the natives, French settlers recognized the value in river travel. Not only was it easier and faster than overland travel, but the Mississippi's vast network of tributaries gave them access to land between the Rockies and the Appalachians. Exploring this way, the French claimed much of the Mississippi basin over the next 100 years.

French trappers and fur traders were the first to settle along the Mississippi, setting up outposts along the river to trade beaver, mink, and otter pelts, and to ship them to Europe for great profits. Ste. Genevieve, Missouri, one of the first European settlements along the Mississippi River, was founded in 1735. Five of the vertical log homes built by French settlers, one dating back to 1770, still stand today.[5] The French had little interest in expanding settlements beyond building a few garrisons, or forts, along the banks, such as Fort Chartres, which still stands near present-day Prairie du Rocher, Illinois.

After their 1763 defeat in the French and Indian War, the French turned over their claim on all land east of the Mississippi to the British. Many French who remained in the New World moved to Louisiana, the closest remaining French-held land. The French integrated so well with the swampland natives that the two become one in a new culture, Creole. Some native swamp dwellers even today speak Creole as their first language, a hybrid of French and ancient tongues of native tribes. World-famous Creole cooking uses French recipes, tailored to use local swamp ingredients like bay leaves, powder made from ground sassafras root, and meats like crawfish, shrimp, and alligator.[6]

In 1783, much of the land east of the Mississippi became the property of the newborn United States. American were a bit wary to settle the Mississippi, however, when their government could only claim its east side. That changed on April 30, 1803, when President Thomas Jefferson paid $15 million to the French emperor Napoleon for rights over all the territory between the

Thomas Jefferson

Mississippi River and the Rocky Mountains. The Louisiana Purchase doubled the young nation's size overnight. It also began a golden age of expansion and exploration for the United States. American explorers Meriwether Lewis and William Clark began their epic trek from the "new" side of the river at St. Louis on May 14 , 1804. American settlers soon followed the brave Lewis and Clark, rushing in to discover new opportunities on both sides of the Mighty Miss.

Jean Lafitte, Pirate Hero of New Orleans

Jean Lafitte

A blacksmith's forge opened on the streets of New Orleans in 1803 as a front for one of the greatest thieves of all time. Jean Lafitte (1776-1823), the mysterious Gentleman Pirate of New Orleans, sold the goods New Orleans's residents needed—food, clothes, furniture, tools, and more—in his own shops, at great discounts to his customers. To the residents of New Orleans, Lafitte was a godsend. To the governors, he was a thief and a traitor who managed to sneak around the ships that charged taxes.

Lafitte made his headquarters on Grand Terre Island in Barataria Bay, where the Mississippi's mouth spills into the Gulf of Mexico. No ship could sail in or out of the Mississippi without Lafitte and his renegades having a first look at it. From their strategic base, they scoured the Caribbean Sea, plundering overloaded Spanish galleons for goods and treasure. Lafitte was especially well-known for his discounted slaves, bought for $300 each in Cuba and sold for $1,200 in the slave markets in New Orleans.[7]

Who was Jean Lafitte? Not an American citizen, yet he loved America and what it stood for. Lafitte was arrested several times, yet repeatedly escaped. He fought side-by-side with Andrew Jackson to defeat the British at the Battle of New Orleans on January 8, 1815, and then turned coat and spied on New Orleans for Spain. After his death off of Galveston Island, Texas in battle with a Spanish galleon, rumors spread that Lafitte had buried treasure on Grand Terre... but none has been found. Yet.

Steamboat races brought excitement up and down the
Mississippi – and drummed up good business for the

CHAPTER 3

Old Man River Connects North and South

America's new expansion brought great excitement to the nation's poor, huddled together on the east coast. Waves of immigrants from Europe—over 30 million between 1836 and 1914—proved to be some of the Upper Mississippi's first and most important permanent settlers.[1] Many of these immigrants had broken their backs as serfs in the Old World, farming as little more than slaves for wealthy landowners. Groups like the Forty-Eighters fought in revolutions in Germany and other European countries in 1848, seeking democracy and religious freedom. These revolutions were defeated and the Forty-Eighters fled. What they could not gain in their home countries they found along the Mississippi River. Their hardened farming hands willingly picked up plows to work their own land. By 1850, immigrants, especially those from Germany and Sweden, had founded many small farms and villages in Minnesota, Wisconsin, Iowa, Illinois, and Missouri. In large part because of their efforts, the Mississippi River Valley became America's main food-producing region from the mid-nineteenth century on.

Though few farmers along the Upper River grew rich on oats, wheat, corn, potatoes, and other fruits and vegetables, they had plenty to feed their families and animals with enough left over to sell for a comfortable profit. In contrast, the warm, sultry climate along the southern Mississippi turned farmland into gold. Valuable cash crops like sugarcane, rice, and cotton grew like wildfire in Tennessee, Arkansas, Mississippi, and Louisiana. By the 1820s, the richest southerners bought up land around their family farms to create plantations, which were too large for a single family to maintain. Many bought slaves imported from Africa to help work the large plantations. The U.S. Census of 1860 counted nearly 1.5 million slaves toiling in states along the Mississippi River, compared to 3.9 million free men. In the cotton-dense state of Mississippi, slaves outnumbered whites.[2]

Ports sprung up along the river to accommodate trade between the north—with its furs, wheat, oats, vegetables, and fruits—and the south, with its cash crops and exports from Europe and beyond. But how did these products get from one port to the next? Canoes could carry two experienced rivermen, but had little room to spare for a sack of grain or a bale of cotton. Between 1786 and 1811, traders along the Mississippi used keelboats.[3] These rivercraft carried cargo on large, flat decks, riding the current downriver to sell in New Orleans.

However, keelboats were heavy and hard to steer on the unpredictable river. And getting to New Orleans was the easy part. To get back home, boatmen switched between rowing against the current, pushing the boat along with a pole stuck in the shallow muck, or throwing a rope ashore and towing the boat, hiking through reedy wetlands. Most river rats chose to sell their keelboats after unloading in New Orleans and walk back home. Either way, the river was well known to robbers and savage natives, all lying in wait to rob the traders blind. Not surprisingly, successful keelboatmen earned a reputation as rough-and-tumble adventure-seekers. River tales tell that the King of the

Keelboatmen camp along the river. A typical keelboat was narrow, around 70 feet long, with a small cabin to house the crew and a few tons of cargo.

Keelboaters was Mike Fink, a braggart, a bully, and a legend with a pistol.

Robert Fulton invented the steamboat in 1807, an engineering marvel that would change life on the Mississippi forever. On December 19, 1811, the *New Orleans* became the first steamboat to enter the Mississippi River, passing New Madrid, Missouri as it left the Ohio River.[4] Suddenly, upriver travel became not just profitable, but safe and relatively easy. Useful and romantic, steamboats opened a world of travel and adventure. Prospective settlers could travel in style from the east, taking all their belongings and family without the backbreaking overland journey. By the 1830s, steamboats regularly chugged up and down the Mississippi carrying cotton and settlers back and forth from New Orleans to St. Louis, or via the Ohio River to Pittsburgh, Pennsylvania. By 1839, the port of New Orleans rivaled that of New York City. St. Louis, Memphis, and Washington, Louisiana, all boomed as important steamboat towns along the river.

Steamboats brought excitement to sleepy river towns. Born in 1835, a boy from Hannibal, Missouri named Samuel Clemens dreamed of

Samuel Clemens (left) sits on a porch with his lifelong friend, John T. Lewis (right). Clemens's white clapboard house still stands in Hannibal, Missouri, as the Mark Twain Boyhood Home and Museum.

working on a steamboat as he grew up. Clemens did become a steamboat captain, and eventually he wrote about his colorful life on the Mississippi with shipmen, travelers, and regular river folk. He published books such as *Tom Sawyer* and *Huckleberry Finn* under the pseudonym Mark Twain, a boatman's term that meant the river was deep enough for ships to pass safely.

Steamboats did have their drawbacks. Navigation could be dangerous, especially along the shallower Upper River. Downed trees and sandbars caused the top-heavy boats to wreck. When the *Tennessee* caught in a snag and sank in 1823, at least 68 passengers drowned.[5] Steamboats occasionally collided with each other, with disastrous results. The boats themselves were prone to explode, loaded with enormous boilers that sometimes could not take the pressure. In 1817, the *Constitution's* boiler burst suddenly, wounding or killing over 30 passengers.[6] Passengers also had to beware of greedy captains who overloaded their boats, sometimes causing the heavy vessels to sink.

FAST FACTS

Origin of Name: "mesipi" – Ojibwe word meaning "big river."

Countries: United States, Canada

Major cities: St. Paul/Minneapolis, Minnesota; St. Louis, Missouri; Memphis, Tennessee; Baton Rouge, Louisiana; New Orleans, Louisiana.

Primary tributaries: Missouri River, Ohio River, Arkansas River.

Secondary sources: Illinois River, Tennessee River, White River, Red River, Yazoo River.

Watershed: The Mississippi drains 1,151,000 square miles (2,981,076 square kilometers), or 41% of the continental United States.[7]

Elevations: 1475 feet (450 meters) at Lake Itasca; 0 feet at the Head of Passes.

Source: Lake Itasca, Minnesota (47°13′05″N 95°12′26″W), and many other creeks and streams.

Mouth: Head of Passes (29.157°N 89.254°W), 95 miles south of New Orleans, which drains into the Gulf of Mexico.

Length: Estimated at 2320 - 2350 miles.[8] The river's path makes constant, small changes, so knowing its exact length is impossible.

Width: From 20 to 30 feet across at its headwaters at Lake Itasca, to over 11 miles across at Lake Winnibigoshish, Minnesota. The river's widest navigable point is 2 miles across at Lake Pepin, on the border between Minnesota and Wisconsin.

Speed: 1.2 miles per hour at Lake Itasca; 3 miles per hour at New Orleans, Louisiana.

In the 1830s, the American railroad boom brought a safer alternative to steamboat travel. Rails could be laid anywhere, even over river-spanning bridges. Trains moved people and freight more efficiently and reliably than steamboats. And trains that kept to the river's banks continued to serve the industries and cities that still relied on the river. However, growing political conflicts between the North and the South hampered railroad construction along the Mississippi River.

When Illinois native Abraham Lincoln was elected president in 1860, the wealthy South could not help but see his anti-slavery speeches as a threat to their lifestyle. Southern farmers required free labor from slaves to keep their plantations running. Mississippi and Louisiana seceded, or broke away from, the United States in January 1861, with Tennessee and Arkansas joining them in May of that year. Missouri followed six months later. With six other southern states, they formed the Confederate States of America, united by their belief that only slavery could keep their way of life alive.

Union General Ulysses S. Grant recognized the importance of controlling the Mississippi River. Union troops quickly took New Orleans, the South's largest city, on April 28, 1862. Vicksburg, Mississippi served as the "Gibraltar of the Confederacy," a major stronghold of the Confederate Army. The city fell to Union troops on July 4, 1863 after a hard-fought 47-day battle, considered by some to be the beginning of the end for the Confederate Army. With the victory at Vicksburg, the Union claimed control of the entire Mississippi River. The Confederate Army surrendered on April 9, 1865, ending the Civil War. No more would slavery stain American soil.

Did you know?

Call letters of radio and TV stations in the United States begin with the letter "W" on the east side of the Mississippi. Stations to the west of the river begin with "K."

Tall Tales

Mike Fink

The Mississippi River Valley became a land of plenty, but only through difficult exploration and back-breaking daily labor. As folks gathered around a fire at the end of a long day, they told each other stories. From these fireside tales arose some of America's best-known folk heroes, real people whose bravery and deeds inspired outrageous stories.

Famous frontiersman Daniel Boone may not have wrestled a bear, or escaped from savage Indians by swinging on vines through the forest while waving his coonskin cap. But Boone did settle along the Ohio River in Kentucky in the 18th century—in what would later be named Boone County after him—and lived his last 20 years in St. Charles County, Missouri along the Mississippi River.

"King of the Keelboaters" Mike Fink may not have been half horse and half alligator, nor ridden a waterfall like a bucking bronco. But everyone who knew him agreed that this 19th century river rat was a muscled sharpshooter extraordinaire, and certainly a braggart.

Stories of Paul Bunyan, the giant lumberjack who worked the forests of the frontier, probably were not based on an actual person. Instead, Bunyan's character reflects the everyday lives of actual lumberjacks, served up as super-sized as his legendary pancake breakfast. Fierce and deadly Minnesota blizzards probably claimed many settlers' lives. Though Bunyan was spared, the 10,000 steps from his blind wanderings formed the lakes of Minnesota. Statues of Paul and his pet, an enormous blue ox named Blue, stand in downtown Bemidji, Minnesota, near Lake Itasca State Park.

The 10th Avenue Bridge lies just downstream of Minneapolis's Falls of St. Anthony. Designed by Norwegian immigrant Kristoffer Oustad in the late 1920s, the bridge was added to the National Register of Historic Places in 1989.

CHAPTER 4

The Modern Mississippi

Many of the world's major cities sprung up because of their closeness to rivers. Rivers held the key to growth and prosperity, with water, food, and irrigation for farming. The biggest cities along the Mississippi arose at special locations along the river. Today, these cities—Minneapolis/St. Paul in Minnesota, St. Louis in Missouri, Memphis in Tennessee, and New Orleans in Louisiana—boast a combined population of almost nine million altogether.[1]

Minneapolis's name comes from "mni," the Dakota word for water. Minneapolis began as a mill town, using St. Anthony's Falls to power wheat and saw mills. The first bridge spanning the Mississippi was built here in 1855. With St. Paul, the state capital across the Mississippi, the Twin Cities (3.5 million) today form the nation's largest urban area between Seattle and Chicago. Minneapolis boasts an active theater community, and is constantly ranked high in literacy, education, and technology.

For nearly 200 years, farmland has dominated Upper River communities. Minnesota leads the nation in producing sugar beets, sweet corn, and green peas. Iowa produces dairy and corn-based ethanol, an important additive to gasoline. Illinois farms yield some of the largest crops of corn and soybeans. Missouri is known for its soybeans, hogs, and cattle. Moline, Illinois was home to inventor John Deere, who invented a special plow blade to farm tough, dense, sticky prairie soil.[2] Comic artist Elzie Crisler Seger, creator of spinach fan Popeye, grew up in the river town of Chester, Illinois.[3]

St. Louis, Missouri (metro population 2,845,298), also known as the Gateway to the West, was founded in 1764 as a French stronghold, nestled strategically near the confluence of the Missouri River with the Mississippi. Interestingly, what we now call the Mississippi is simply what French explorers chose to travel in the 17th century because their

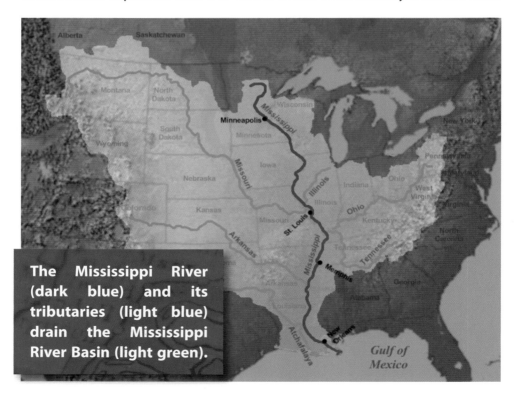

The Mississippi River (dark blue) and its tributaries (light blue) drain the Mississippi River Basin (light green).

The St. Louis Gateway Arch

route began in Canada. Measuring the Mississippi along the course that the Missouri takes—from one of the Missouri's sources, the Jefferson River in Montana to the Gulf of Mexico—would make it the fourth-longest river in the world, at 3,710 miles (5,971 kilometers).[4]

From humble defensive and agricultural roots, St. Louis sprouted into a great city of industry and business. By the 1860s, traffic in its bustling ports rivaled that of New York City. In 1874, the 6,442-foot-long Eads Bridge—the longest arch bridge in the world at the time—spanned the Mississippi to connect St. Louis with East St. Louis. In 1904, St. Louis hosted the World's Fair. The city's most familiar landmark, the Gateway Arch, completed in October 1965, sits along the west bank of the Mississippi.

The city of Memphis (metro population 1,316,100) was founded in the 1820s, built on the bluff where Hernando de Soto first sighted the Mississippi. Named after the capital of ancient Egypt, Memphis became a major port city in the 19th century, largely due to its protected location high above the Mississippi's floodplain. Memphis's important location during the slavery era positioned it to become a world leader in the cotton and wood trade.

At the heart of the South, Memphis is a center of African-American culture. The National Civil Rights Museum is located at the Lorraine Motel, where Dr. Martin Luther King, Jr. was shot to death on the balcony of Room 306-7.[5] Fears and worries from poverty and racism found an outlet through a new kind of music, the blues, which was born in Memphis. Memphis native and educated musician W.C. Handy didn't mean to set the world on fire when he published his song, "Memphis Blues," in 1912. Considered by many to be the first official blues song, it blended black folk music with ragtime, and soon made the music clubs on Beale Street—with its many music clubs—a household name. Blues legends born and raised on Handy's blues

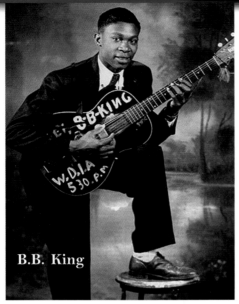

B.B. King

included Memphis natives Muddy Waters, Robert Johnson, B.B. King, and later rock 'n roll pioneers such as Jerry Lee Lewis. The King of rock 'n roll, Elvis Presley, was discovered in August 1953 at Memphis's Sun Records. At today's citywide festival, "Memphis in May," festivalgoers can listen to world-class music at the Beale Street Music Festival, and pig out on soul food in Memphis's world-record-holding Barbeque Cooking Contest.

Like Memphis, Baton Rouge, Louisiana (metro population 802,484) enjoys a protected location on a bluff above the river. Even though Baton Rouge lies 100 miles upriver from the Gulf of Mexico, its waters run so deep that the city's port accommodates oceangoing vessels. Its importance in trade made it a natural choice as the capital city of Louisiana, where proud residents built the nation's tallest capitol building.[6]

Native American, French, and Spanish history have mingled in New Orleans (metro population 1,235,650) to create a true American original. New Orleans began as a port, laid out by French Army in 1721. A 90-block section bordered by the river known as the French Quarter preserves both French and Spanish architecture. New Orleans's Bourbon Street is world-famous for its creole food and Dixieland jazz music, and especially for its Mardi Gras festival, held every year just before the start of Lent for the Christian church. In addition to serving as one of the largest and busiest ports in the world, New Orleans's economy also runs on oil. Helicopters buzz through the city, carrying petroleum geologists, engineers, and rig workers to oil derricks in the Gulf.

Today, New Orleans struggles to rebuild after devastating floods from Hurricane Katrina nearly destroyed it in 2005. Though flooding

Katrina flood

dangers exist for all urban areas along the Mississippi, New Orleans's location near the Gulf of Mexico helps place it in the worst situation for flood management. Half of the city lies below sea level, even below the level of the river. To keep out the river and the sea, New Orleans residents built the first levees—manmade dirt walls that raised the river's banks—in 1726. By 1812, levees lined the city's banks, some as high as 40 feet. Leaks and bursts were inevitable as the river sought natural relief, drowning buildings, crops, and people each time. However, by the early 18th century, the area had already become popular with businesses and residents. With money invested in area businesses, agriculture, buildings, schools, and streets, people chose to fight the river. They have been fighting ever since.

Modern cities' needs have changed. We now use roads and airports, instead of river trade and travel, to connect us to our daily needs for food and goods. Today, cities view their rivers more like parks or scenery than an integral part of life. Along the Upper River, the Mississippi seems like a great place to hunt elk or deer. Fishermen chase after "river cat," enormous catfish that can tip the scales at 200 pounds. Southerners make a good living catching crawfish, shrimp, and even alligator for meat.

It seems easy, then to ignore the strain that growing cities put on the river's environment. New construction of houses and roads fills in wetlands and cuts down forests that wildlife use for habitats. Half of the Mississippi's natural wetlands have disappeared, with over 80 percent gone in Iowa, Missouri, and Illinois.[7] Whole ecosystems depend on insects that call these wetlands home, which provide an important food source for river fish as well as for local and migratory birds.

For a long time, factories used the river as a dumping ground for their waste. The city of St. Louis dumped 300 million gallons of raw sewage directly into the river until its sewers were updated in 1970.[8] Nearly one-third of the 300 million pounds of toxic chemicals dumped into the river each year are dumped between New Orleans and Baton Rouge. Mercury and polychlorinated biphenyls (PCBs)—products of industrial waste—have been found at high levels in the Mississippi's water, as well as in the bodies of its fish and wildlife. Trash and chemicals in the river affect the water's quality, important to plants, animals, and the communities along the river that rely on purified river water for drinking.

Agriculture along the Mississippi River has perhaps made the biggest impact on the river's health. Farms depend on the river's water and the fertile soil nearby. But in return, modern farming practices pollute the river with fertilizers, pesticides, and herbicides carried off the land by rain or irrigation. Popular weedkillers like atrazine and metolachlor can be toxic to fish, birds, and aquatic life. Fertilizers encourage algae to grow so rapidly that it consumes the river oxygen needed by fish and other animals. Without oxygen, the Mississippi's water becomes a dead zone, one that balloons out into the Gulf of Mexico.[9]

The Mississippi's residents are beginning to clean up their act. Sewage treatment and releasing facilities have improved. The strongest pesticides have been banned or restricted. The Federal Clean Water Act of 1972 encouraged companies to take responsibility for their environmental impacts. When Shell Oil was fined $1.5 million for pollution at its Missouri plant, other companies took notice. Industrial giants such as Dow, Monsanto, and 3M with factories along the Mississippi have pledged to release fewer contaminants. With help from increasingly aware local residents, people are learning how to live alongside the Big Muddy in the modern world.

Cleaning up
The Big Muddy

Chad Pregracke

Chad Pregracke grew up in the small town of Hampton, Illinois, in a family that loved the river. His brother became a commercial fisherman on the Mississippi. Chad himself worked part-time as a shell diver, fisherman, and barge hand during his high school and college years.

When his work kept him away from home, he loved to camp on the Mississippi's islands. Living and working on the river, Chad couldn't help but notice the garbage, from cheeseburger wrappers to La-Z-Boys—literally everything, including kitchen sinks—carelessly dumped in the river. He called local, state, and national officials, trying to find out who was responsible for cleaning up the river. Their silence was his answer—no one.

Chad decided to take action. In 1997, the 22-year-old went to the river with a garbage bag and picked up the Mississippi's garbage himself, one piece at a time. The enthusiastic young man soon recruited an army of volunteers to help. The next year, Chad founded Living Lands and Waters, a non-profit organization dedicated to cleaning up the Mississippi. Since then, Chad and over 60,000 volunteers have gathered more than six million pounds of trash, using a small fleet of boats, other watercraft and trucks to expand their clean-up to include other U.S. rivers.

For his efforts, Chad has received many awards and honors, most notably the Samuel S. Beard Award in 2002, a prestigious national medal for public service by young people.

A New Orleans street lies underwater during the Great Flood of 1927. The untamed Mississippi overran 27,000 square miles of the American South, with damages exceeding today's equivalent of $1 billion.

Can You Control a Strong Brown God?

The rain began in the Upper Mississippi River Valley in August. By September 1, smaller streams were overcome, drowning towns from Carroll, Iowa to Peoria, Illinois. After 15 inches of rain fell in Sioux City, Iowa, in early October, the Mississippi River swelled to knock out bridges and wash away railroad tracks. In mid-December, new storms brought six inches of rain to Arkansas. The river gauge at Vicksburg, Mississippi read 40 feet at a time of year when people were used to seeing the zero mark. On January 1, the Mississippi reached flood stage at Cairo, Illinois, and yet the rain continued to fall. Downpours in mid-January along the lower Mississippi, coupled with heavy snowfall on the upper river, kept river gauges between Cairo and New Orleans at flood stage for over 150 days. On April 15, downtown New Orleans stood under 4 feet of water from rainfall alone. Only the carefully constructed levees protected homes, land, and lives from the record-breaking two million cubic feet of

Men in Yazoo City, Mississippi can only watch helplessly as the Mississippi's 1927 floodwaters reach their rails and cotton bales.

rainwater that the Mississippi carried past every second. Nervous crews built the levees higher with sandbags in hopes that height would buy them enough time for the river to calm down.

On April 16, 1,200 feet of levee collapsed at Dorena, Missouri, flooding 175,000 acres of land. Five days later, 3,960 feet of levee crumbled at Mounds Landing, Mississippi. The Mississippi rushed through the breach with the force of Niagara Falls, turning an area 60 miles east and 90 miles south into a rainwater ocean. Homes in Yazoo City, Mississippi, 75 miles away, stood roof-deep in water.[1] Soggy levees failed throughout the South over the next two weeks. At its highest-ever capacity, the Mississippi poured an average of 2,345,000 cubic feet per second into the Gulf, enough to fill the Louisiana Superdome in 45 seconds.[2] The total flooding left over one million acres of land underwater.

Though this may sound like a headline from 2011, this record-breaking flood actually occurred in 1927. Nearly 1,000 people drowned in the raging waters or died of exposure from the chilly spring weather. The Red Cross built tent cities to feed, clothe, and house over 700,000

Southerners who had lost everything but their lives. The loss of valuable farmland, homes, and businesses, added to clean-up efforts, amounted to $1 billion in damages.[3] Flooding on the Mississippi is nothing new. Most of the time, the Mississippi's banks are high enough to contain its waters, and the river can go for years without flooding. But in years with heavy winter snows or spring rains, the overloaded river floods.

The Native Americans learned quickly to respect the river's power to flood and built on high land—either naturally occurring bluffs or hills, or their own manmade mounds. They lived in small shelters that could be moved or rebuilt if floodwaters threatened. They also did not depend solely on crops to survive, so if floods washed their farms away they would not starve. When American settlers came in the 19th century, they built permanent stone structures and relied on their farms to feed their families, just as they had done back home. Instead of moving with the river, settlers left themselves no choice but to try—and sometimes fail—to control the river.

The strategy in current operation, passed down from the Mississippi's settlers, has been to build levees along the river's banks to protect the lands from floods. Levees protected New Orleans as early as 1726. In 1850, the U.S. government claimed 32,000 square miles of riverbank land to build levees and drain swamps in hopes of taming the river. Some engineers proposed building outlets or cutoffs to make the Mississippi run straighter—and therefore faster—to the Gulf. Chief U.S. Army Engineer Andrew Humphreys, however, pushed hard to continue building levees. His strategy has been in place ever since 1861.

After the Great Flood of 1927, the U.S. Congress took further steps to ensure that such devastation would not happen again. The Flood Control Act of 1928 authorized the Army Corps of Engineers to better manage the Mississippi River. Throughout the 1930s and 1940s, the Corps created cutoffs—shortening the river by over 150 miles—to make the Mississippi run more quickly to its end.[4] They constructed four spillways, or large walls with removable gates that guard the river's borders: the Birds Point Floodway near New Madrid, Missouri; the

Morganza Spillway near Morganza, Mississippi, the West Atchafalaya Floodway in Louisiana, and the Bonne Carré Spillway 22 miles upriver of New Orleans.

The spillways can be opened up in the event of catastrophic floods, lowering the height of the river near major economic centers like Memphis, Baton Rouge, and New Orleans, by flooding low-lying rural land. The Corps built the Old River Control, enormous solid concrete and steel gates, that diverted 600,000 cubic feet per second to the Atchafalaya River.[5] Most visibly, the Corps also built 3,787 miles of levees along the Mississippi and its tributaries, including tall, continuous levees that cage in 1,108 miles of river channel between Cape Girardeau, Missouri and Venice, Louisiana.[6] The Corps continues to dredge the lower river—digging out the river bed—to increase the river's capacity.

However, after 70 years and nearly $13 billion dollars of river improvements, the Mississippi still refuses to be completely contained. Though never as badly as in 1927, the Mississippi has flooded catastrophically several times in recent history, most notably in 1844, 1951, 1993, 2008, and 2011.

Environmental scientists also worry that increased urbanization makes the Mississippi more likely to flood. Between 1993 and 2001—a period of less than eight years—four floods occurred that should only happen once every 100 years or even more. As cities sprawl out along the river, bare soil that naturally absorbs rainfall gets covered over with asphalt. The rain has nowhere to go but to the swelling river.

Today, residents are learning to work with, instead of against, the river. In East Dubuque, Illinois, the government closed off low-lying neighborhoods and bulldozed houses in an effort to leave the land to return to its natural state as a marsh. After the town of Valmyer, Illinois was destroyed by the 1993 floods, residents voted to relocate the town to a nearby bluff high above the river.[7] There are no easy answers, but with renewed understanding, perhaps people can live with respect for the Father of Waters.

The Atchafalaya River

The Atchafalaya floods a forest.

The Atchafalaya River through Louisiana is the Mississippi's only major distributary. The Atcha-falaya—meaning "long river" in Choctaw—branches off of the Mississippi at Simmesport, near where the Red River meets them both. The Atchafalaya, which has a total length of 137 miles (220 kilometers) is actually a more natural outlet for the Mississippi's water. It carves a shorter, steeper, faster route to the Gulf through the heart of Creole country. It seems inevitable that the Mississippi's delta would move, as it has about every 1,000 years, adopting the Atchafalaya's outlet south of Morgan City.[8]

To the Mississippi's relatively new human neighbors, however, such a change threatens serious social disaster. Agriculture along the Lower River would literally dry up, as would the economies of Baton Rouge and New Orleans at a cost of nearly $300 million per day.[9] The small bayou communities along the Atchafalaya would be underwater, forced to move, or face flooding.

To partly dam the Atchafalaya, the U.S. Army Corps of Engineers completed the billion-dollar Old River Control Structure (ORCS) in 1963, which allows only 30 percent of the Mississippi's flow into the Atchafalaya. Many experts believe, however, that it is only a matter of time before nature takes its course. In 1973, the Mississippi's floodwaters nearly dug the ORCS out from its base. ORCS's gates were opened for the first time in 2011, soaking the Morganza Spillway but preventing the river from flooding Baton Rouge and New Orleans.

Chapter 1 Big River: What's in a Name?

1. Stephen E. Ambrose, *The Mississippi and the Making of a Nation: From the Louisiana Purchase to Today* (Washington, D.C.: National Geographic, 2002), p.9.
2. United States National Parks Service, "Mississippi River National Recreational Area." http://www.nps.gov/miss/index.htm.
3. Troy Taylor, "The Curse of Kaskaskia—Illinois' Lost Capital." Prairieghosts.com. http://www.prairieghosts.com/kaskaskia.html.
4. Readers' Digest Association, *See the U.S.A. the Easy Way: 136 Loop Tours to 1200 Great Places* (Pleasantville, NY: Readers' Digest Association, 1995), p. 136.
5. Missouri Department of Natural Resources, "Geologic Hazards in Missouri." http://www.dnr.mo.gov/geology/geosrv/geores/geohazhp.htm.

Chapter 2 Father of Waters: Early History and Explanation

1. Stephen E. Ambrose, *The Mississippi and the Making of a Nation: From the Louisiana Purchase to Today* (Washington, D.C.: National Geographic, 2002), p. 9.
2. George R. Milner, *The Moundbuilders: Ancient Peoples of Eastern North America* (London: Thames and Hudson, 2004), p. 13.
3. Robert S. Weddle, "ALVAREZ DE PINEDA, ALONSO," Handbook of Texas Online, Texas State Historical Association. http://www.tshaonline.org/handbook/online/articles/fal72.
4. Father Jacques Marquette, "Voyages du P. Jacques Marquette, 1673-1675," The Jesuit Relations and Allied Documents 1610-1791. http://puffin.creighton.edu/jesuit/relations/relations_59.html.
5. Readers' Digest Association, *See the U.S.A. the Easy Way: 136 Loop Tours to 1200 Great Places* (Pleasantville, NY: Readers' Digest Association, 1995), p. 196.
6. Alton Brown, *Feasting on Asphalt* (New York: Stewart, Tabori, and Chang, 2005), p. 53.
7. Joseph Geringer, "Jean Lafitte: Gentleman Pirate Of New Orleans," truTV.com. http://www.trutv.com/library/crime/gangsters_outlaws/cops_others/lafitte.

Chapter 3 Old Man River Connects the North and South

1. Irial Glynn, "Emigration Across the Atlantic: Irish, Italians and Swedes compared, 1800-1950," European History Online, June 6, 2011. http://www.ieg-ego.eu/en/threads/europe-on-the-road/economic-migration/irial-glynn-emigration-across-the-atlantic-irish-italians-and-swedes-compared-1800-1950
2. United States Census, 1860. http://www.census.gov/prod/www/abs/decennial/1860.html.
3. James T. Lloyd, *Lloyd's Steamboat Directory* (Cincinnati, Ohio: James T. Lloyd & Co., 1856), p. 40.
4. Mary Helen Dohan, *Mr. Roosevelt's Steamboat: The First Steamboat to Travel the Mississippi* (Gretna, Louisiana: Pelican Publishing Company, 2004), p. 5.
5. Lloyd, *Lloyd's Steamboat Directory,* p. 61.
6. Ibid., p. 57.
7. Mississippi River-Gulf of Mexico Watershed Nutrient Task Force, "The Mississippi-Atchafalaya River Basin." United States Environmental Protection Agency. http://water.epa.gov/type/watersheds/named/msbasin/marb.cfmnumber 6
8. United States National Parks Service, "Mississippi River National Recreational Area." http://www.nps.gov/miss/index.htm

Chapter 4 The Modern Mississippi

1. United States Census, 2010.
   http://2010.census.gov/2010census/
2. Alton Brown, *Feasting on Asphalt* (New York: Stewart, Tabori, and Chang, 2005), 158.
3. Ibid., p. 114.
4. J.C. Kammerer, "Largest Rivers in the United States." U.S. Geological Survey, May, 1990.
   http://pubs.usgs.gov/of/1987/ofr87-242/
5. Readers' Digest Association, *See the U.S.A. the Easy Way: 136 Loop Tours to 1200 Great Places* (Pleasantville, NY: Readers' Digest Association, 1995), p. 136.
6. Ibid., p. 171.
7. Michael Grunwald, "Disasters All, but Not as Natural as You Think," *Washington Post,* May 6, 2001.
   http://newnet2000.de/Info-Pool/Special_Issues/Waterways/Materials/materials.html
8. "The States: Changing the Face." *Time,* February 23, 1962.
   http://www.time.com/time/magazine/article/0,9171,829463,00.html
9. Dubravko Justic, Nancy N. Rabalais, and R. Eugene Turner. "Simulated responses of the Gulf of Mexico hypoxia to variations in climate and anthropogenic nutrient loading." Journal of Marine Systems, vol. 42, pp.115-126, 2003.

Chapter 5 Can You Control a Strong, Brown God?

1. Chana Gazit, "American Experience: Fatal Flood," PBS Online.
   http://www.pbs.org/wgbh/amex/flood/index.html
2. "Mississippi River Anatomy," America's Wetland Resource Center.
   http://www.americaswetlandresources.com/background_facts/detailedstory/MississippiRiverAnatomy.html.
3. John M. Barry, *Rising Tide: The Great Mississippi Flood of 1927 and How It Changed America* (New York: Simon & Schuster, 1998), p. 286.
4. "Man vs. Nature: The Great Mississippi Flood of 1927," *National Geographic News,* May 1, 2001. http://news.nationalgeographic.com/news/2001/05/0501_river4.html
5. Paul Rioux, "Flow of Mississippi River floodwaters through the Morganza spillway to increase gradually," New Orleans Times-Picayune, May 14, 2011.
   http://www.nola.com/environment/index.ssf/2011/05/flow_of_mississippi_river_floo.html
6. United States Army Corps of Engineers, Mississippi Valley Division. http://www.mvd.usace.army.mil/
7. "Valmeyer, Illinois," Operation Fresh Start. http://www.freshstart.ncat.org/case/valmeyer.htm.
8. John McPhee, "The Control of Nature: Atchafalaya," *New Yorker,* February 23, 1987.
   http://www.newyorker.com/archive/1987/02/23/1987_02_23_039_TNY_CARDS_000347146
9. Rioux, "Flow of Mississippi River floodwaters through the Morganza spillway to increase gradually."
   http://www.nola.com/environment/index.ssf/2011/05/flow_of_mississippi_river_floo.html

Ambrose, Stephen E. *The Mississippi and the Making of a Nation: From the Louisiana Purchase to Today.* Washington, D.C.: National Geographic, 2002.

Barry, John M. *Rising Tide: The Great Mississippi Flood of 1927 and How It Changed America.* New York: Simon & Schuster, 1998.

Botkin, B.A. *A Treasury of Mississippi River Folklore.* New York: Crown Publishers, Inc., 1955.

Brown, Alton. *Feasting on Asphalt,* New York: Stewart, Tabori, and Chang, 2005.

Dohan, Mary Helen. *Mr. Roosevelt's Steamboat: The First Steamboat to Travel the Mississippi.* Gretna, Louisiana: Pelican Publishing Company, 2004.

Gazit, Chana. "American Experience: Fatal Flood." PBS Online, http://www.pbs.org/wgbh/amex/flood/index.html

Geringer, Joseph. "Jean Lafitte: Gentleman Pirate Of New Orleans." truTV.com, http://www.trutv.com/library/crime/gangsters_outlaws/cops_others/lafitte

Glynn, Irial. "Emigration Across the Atlantic: Irish, Italians and Swedes compared, 1800-1950." European History Online, June 6, 2011.

Grunwald, Michael. "Disasters All, but Not as Natural as You Think." *Washington Post,* May 6, 2001.

Heacox, Kim, K.M. Kostyal, Paul Robert Walker, and Mel White. *Exploring the Great Rivers of North America.* Washington, D.C.: National Geographic Society, 1999.

Justic, Dubravko, Nancy N. Rabalais, and R. Eugene Turner. "Simulated responses of the Gulf of Mexico hypoxia to variations in climate and anthropogenic nutrient loading." *Journal of Marine Systems,* vol. 42, pp.115-126, 2003.

Kammerer, J.C. "Largest Rivers in the United States." United States Geological Survey, Water Resources Division. May 1990. http://pubs.usgs.gov/of/1987/ofr87-242/

Living Lands and Waters
http://www.livinglandsandwaters.org/

Lloyd, James T. *Lloyd's Steamboat Directory.* Cincinnati, Ohio: James T. Lloyd & Co., 1856.

Marquette, Father Jacques. "Voyages du P. Jacques Marquette, 1673-1675". The Jesuit Relations and Allied Documents 1610-1791, http://puffin.creighton.edu/jesuit/relations/relations_59.html

McPhee, John. "The Control of Nature: Atchafalaya." *New Yorker,* February 23, 1987.
http://www.newyorker.com/archive/1987/02/23/1987_02_23_039_TNY_CARDS_000347146

Milner, George R. *The Moundbuilders: Ancient Peoples of Eastern North America.* London: Thames and Hudson, 2004.

"Mississippi River Anatomy." America's Wetland Resource Center. http://www.americaswetlandresources.com/background_facts/detailedstory/MississippiRiverAnatomy.html

Mississippi River-Gulf of Mexico Watershed Nutrient Task Force. "The Mississippi-Atchafalaya River Basin." United States Environmental Protection Agency.
http://water.epa.gov/type/watersheds/named/msbasin/marb.cfm

Missouri Department of Natural Resources. "Geologic Hazards in Missouri." http://www.dnr.mo.gov/geology/geosrv/geores/geohazhp.htm

Operation Fresh Start. "Valmeyer, Illinois." http://www.freshstart.ncat.org/case/valmeyer.htm

"Quiet Beginning Heralded Nation's Worst Flood in 1993." *NOAA Magazine,* April 2003.
http://www.noaanews.noaa.gov/stories/s1125.htm

Raban, Jonathan. *Old Glory: An American Voyage.* New York: Simon & Schuster, 1981.

Readers' Digest Association. *See the U.S.A. the Easy Way: 136 Loop Tours to 1200 Great Places.* Pleasantville, NY: Readers' Digest Association, 1995.

Rioux, Paul. "Flow of Mississippi River floodwaters through the Morganza spillway to increase gradually." *New Orleans Times-Picayune,* May 14, 2011.
http://www.nola.com/environment/index.ssf/2011/05/flow_of_mississippi_river_floo.html

Sandlin, Lee. *Wicked River: The Mississippi When It Last Ran Wild.* New York: Pantheon Books, 2010.

Taylor, Troy. "The Curse of Kaskaskia – Illinois' Lost Capital." Prairieghosts.com.

http://www.prairieghosts.com/kaskaskia.html

Twain, Mark. *Life on the Mississippi.* New York: Harper & Brothers, 1917.

United States Census, 1860. http://www.census.gov/prod/www/abs/decennial/1860.html

United States Census, 2010.
    http://2010.census.gov/2010census/

United States National Parks Service. "Mississippi River National Recreational Area." http://www.nps.gov/miss/index.htm

Weddle, Robert S. "ALVAREZ DE PINEDA, ALONSO." Handbook of Texas Online, Texas State Historical Association, http://www.tshaonline.org/handbook/online/articles/fal72

Weil, Tom. Hippocrene U.S.A. Guide to America's Heartland: A Travel Guide to the Back Roads of Illinois, Indiana, Iowa and Missouri. New York: Hippocrene Books, 1989.

FURTHER READING

Books

Aretha, David. *La Salle: French Explorer of the Mississippi.* Berkeley Heights, New Jersey: Enslow Pubishers, 2009.

Johnson, Robin. *The Mississippi: America's Mighty River.* New York: Crabtree Publishing Co., 2010.

Lourie, Peter. *Mississippi River: A Journey Down the Father of Waters.* Honesdale, Pennsylvania: Boyd's Mill Press, 2002.

Kent, Deborah. *The Great Mississippi Flood of 1927.* New York: Children's Press, 2009.

Osborne, Mary Pope. *A Good Night for Ghosts.* New York: Random House, 2010.

Rasmussen, R. Kent. *Mark Twain for Kids: His Life & Times,* 21 Activities. Chicago: Chicago Review Press, 2004.

Twain, Mark. *The Adventures of Tom Sawyer: Sterling Illustrated Edition.* New York: Sterling Publishing, 2010.

On the Internet

Experience Mississippi River – the Official Site for Mississippi River Travel
    http://www.experiencemississippiriver.com/

Living Lands and Waters
    http://www.livinglandsandwaters.org/

The Mark Twain Boyhood Home and Museum
    http://www.marktwainmuseum.org/

Mississippi National River and Recreation Area – National Parks Service
    http://www.nps.gov/miss/riverfacts.htm

Mississippi River Home Page
    http://www.greatriver.com/

Mississippi River – Free Geography Games and Activities for Kids
    http://www.wartgames.com/themes/geography/mississippiriver.html

Telling River Stories
    http://www.riverstories.umn.edu/

PHOTO CREDITS: All photos—cc-by-sa-2.0. Every effort has been made to locate all copyright holders of material used in this book. If any errors or omissions have occurred, corrections will be made in future editions of the book.

bayou (BYE-you) – A bog or marsh found at the outlet of a river

bluff (BLUHF) – A steep cliff along a body of water

cut-off (CUHT-awff) – A river route that takes a different, shorter path

distributary (diss-TRIBB-you-tarry) – The opposite of tributary; a stream that drains water away from a main channel

levee (LEV-ee) – A manmade hill or mound built along the bank of a body of water to protect the surrounding land from floods

meander (mee-AN-duhr) – The snake-like, side-to-side path carved by slow-moving rivers

oxbow lake (OX-boh LAKE) – A U-shaped lake formed when a river cuts off its own bend

plantation (plan-TAY-shun) – A farm so large that it requires additional laborers

portage (POHR-tehj) – To move a boat over dry land from one body of water to another

pseudonym (SOO-duh-nim) – A false name

sharecropper (SHARE-crop-uhr) – A farm laborer working on land belonging to another person and who has agreed to pay some of the harvest as rent

secede (suh-SEED) – To withdraw from a political union

serf (SURF) – laborer who is bound to land belonging to a lord or other high official and who has few rights

urbanization (uhr-ban-uh-ZAY-shun) – Becoming developed like a city

watershed (WAH-tuhr-shed) – The region drained by a river

Index

ABOUT THE AUTHOR

Claire O'Neal has written over two dozen books with Mitchell Lane. She holds degrees in English and biology from Indiana University, and a Ph.D. in chemistry from the University of Washington. Claire grew up in Illinois and Kentucky, never more than an hour's drive from the Mighty Miss. Though she currently lives in Delaware with her husband and sons, she still makes it back to the old river town of Cape Girardeau, Missouri to visit family.